— BOOK 1

GOODNIGHT
Stories and Rhymes

Brown Watson

ENGLAND

ROUND AND ROUND THE GARDEN

Round and round the garden
Like a teddy bear.
One step, two steps,
Tickle me under there.

Round and round the haystack
Went the little mouse.
One step, two steps,
In his little house.

GEORGIE PORGIE

Georgie Porgie, pudding and pie,
Kissed the girls and made them cry;
When the boys came out to play,
Georgie Porgie ran away.

LITTLE JACK HORNER

Little Jack Horner sat in a corner,
Eating his Christmas pie;
He put in his thumb,
And pulled out a plum,
And said "What a good boy am I!"

LAVENDER'S BLUE

Lavender's blue, dilly, dilly,
Lavender's green;
When I am King, dilly, dilly,
You shall be Queen.

Call up your men, dilly, dilly,
Set them to work,
Some to the plough, dilly, dilly,
Some to the cart.

Some to make hay, dilly, dilly,
Some to thresh corn,
While you and I, dilly, dilly,
Keep ourselves warm.

I LOVE LITTLE PUSSY

I love little pussy,
Her coat is so warm.
And if I don't hurt her
She'll do me no harm.

TWO LITTLE DUCKS

Two little ducks that I once knew,
Fat ducks, skinny ducks,
There were two.

But the one little duck
With the feathers on his back,
He led the other
With a quack, quack, quack.

TOMMY TUCKER

Little Tommy Tucker
Sang for his supper;
What shall we give him?
White bread and butter.
How shall he cut it without any knife?
How will he marry, without any wife?

HARK, HARK

Hark, hark, the dogs do bark,
The beggars are coming to town;
Some in rags and some in jags,
And some in velvet gowns.

Katie
and the Carnival

Katie loved Carnival Week! Fairy
lights and pretty decorations
hung everywhere. Everyone in
Honeybridge was looking forward
to the fancy dress races around the
streets, singing and dancing in the
Town Centre, pet shows, a fun fair,
and – best of all – the Carnival
Parade along the High Street!

"I thought we'd have a float this year!" smiled Miss Croft, Katie's Play School Teacher.
"What's a float?" asked Katie.
"It's what you ride on for the Carnival Parade!" said Doreen Maggs.

"My cousin Glenda is the Carnival Queen," she went on, "so I'm going to be the Carnival Princess! I've got a dress that reaches right down to my ankles, AND I'm having a cloak AND a crown!"

Katie tried hard not to listen.
Nobody liked Doreen much –
mostly because she was just always
telling everyone what she thought
they hadn't done, what they ought
to do, and how she could do it
better!

Soon, Miss Croft was showing them
how to crumple lots of newspapers
to make enough pretty flowers to
turn Mr. Pegg's trailer into the Play
School carnival float!
"When we paint them,"she said,
"they'll look really nice!"

Only Doreen Maggs did not join in the fun.

"We're having bigger flowers than those on the Carnival Queen's float!" she kept saying. "AND lots of shiny streamers! AND great, big balloons!"

"It sounds lovely, Doreen!" smiled Miss Croft. Then, she sighed. "It's a shame we can't have something like that on our float – something to make sure everyone notices us in the parade."

They had all been working so hard, nobody noticed it was time to go home. Miss Croft was pleased when both Katie's Daddy and Darren's Daddy, Mr. Wood, stayed to help with the tidying-up!

And still the talk went on about the Carnival and the Play School float! "I could let you have a bouncy castle," suggested Mr. Wood. "Then Katie and her friends can bounce all through the parade!"

It sounded like a lovely idea!
"That would make our float look
really special," smiled Miss Croft. "If
you're sure it's no trouble...."
"No trouble at all!" said Mr. Wood.
"I will bring it along myself!"

All that week, Katie and her friends made lots and lots of paper flowers. Then, on the evening before the parade, Mr. Pegg brought his truck and trailer round to the back of the Play School Hall.

Miss Croft showed them how to thread the flowers on to string to make the garlands which would hang all around the truck and trailer. Katie couldn't wait to see the bouncy castle in the middle!

The next day, Katie's Mummy helped her to get ready, and they set off for the Town Centre. Lots of people were there already, waiting for the parade to begin.

"There's Mr. Wood!" shouted Katie. "Look, Mummy! He's got our bouncy castle!" She could see Darren and Suzy helping Mr. Wood to blow the castle up.

"A bit more air inside," puffed Mr.
Wood, "then we'll load the castle on
to the float. We can finish pumping
it up, once it's in place! Grab a
rope and help me please, Katie!"

31

What happened next, nobody quite knew. Either Mr. Wood's pumping machine started to go wrong, or someone let go of one of the ropes, or there was a sudden gust of wind....

But the bouncy castle lifted itself off the ground and began rising up into the the air!

"Hold on, Katie!" cried Mr. Wood, scrambling towards her. "Don't let go of the rope!"

"What is all the shouting about?" came another voice, someone they all knew. "I thought you were all coming to see the Carnival Queen's float before we start leading the parade to the park!"

Then, Doreen Maggs looked up and saw the bottom of the bouncy castle, stuck in a tree.

"Where did you get that giant balloon?" she screamed. "Our float is the one that ought to have giant balloons!"

Next minute, she had snatched the
rope from Katie's hand!
"Now, you know –" she began, her
voice becoming a high-pitched wail,
as both her feet left the ground at
once! Everybody started laughing!

"Help! Help!" screamed Doreen.
"Help, somebody! I – I'm floating
away!"
Miss Croft and Mr. Wood tried to
get the rope and pull her down, but
it was just out of their reach!

"Aaaagh!" screamed Doreen Maggs.
"Aaagh! I want to come down!"
There was a jerk, and Doreen
floated up a few more inches! Then
BANG! A sharp twig had made a
hole in the bouncy castle!

The bang made Doreen let go of the rope. She fell into Mr. Pegg's trailer!

"Ow-ow!" she shouted. "I – I'm hurt!"

"What?" laughed Mr. Pegg. "When you and the bouncy castle came down together?"

"I – I've got to go back to the Carnival Queen!" she wailed, looking down at her dirty dress and shoes. "She's already leading the parade!" said someone in the crowd. "You'd best go on the Play School Float."

Thanks to Mr. Wood, another
bouncy castle arrived just in
time. Katie and her friends had a lovely
time, bouncing up and down and
waving to everyone all the way to
the park!

SIX LITTLE MICE

Six little mice sat down to spin;
Pussy passed by, and she peeped in.
What are you doing, my little men?
Weaving coats for gentlemen.

CHERRY STONES

Cherry stones, cherry stones,
Cherry stones upon the plate.
Make a wish, will it come true?
To get the answer, all you do,
Is say the words with fine endeavour –
'This year. Next year. Some time. Never.'

PRETTY MAID

Pretty maid, pretty maid,
Where have you been?
Gathering roses
To give to the Queen.

44

Pretty maid, pretty maid,
What gave she you?
She gave me a diamond
As big as my shoe.

LITTLE MISS MUFFET

Little Miss Muffet
Sat on her tuffet,
Eating her curds and whey;
There came a big spider,
Who sat down beside her,
And frightened Miss Muffet away.

DAVY DUMPLING

Davy Davy Dumpling,
Boil him in the pot;
Sugar him and butter him,
And eat him while he's hot.

LITTLE BOY BLUE

Little Boy Blue,
Come blow your horn,
The sheep's in the meadow,
The cow's in the corn.

Where is the boy
Who looks after the sheep?
He's under the haystack,
Fast asleep!

ORANGES AND LEMONS

Oranges and lemons,
Say the bells of St. Clement's.
You owe me five farthings,
Say the bells of St. Martin's.

When will you pay me?
Say the bells of Old Bailey.
When I grow rich,
Say the bells of Shoreditch.

When will that be?
Say the bells of Stepney.
I'm sure I don't know,
Says the great bell of Bow.

PEASE PUDDING

Pease pudding hot,
Pease pudding cold,
Pease pudding in the pot,
Nine days old.

53

Teddy
Goes to School

It was a beautiful day and Billy and Bella Bear had been playing with Teddy in his back garden. They had splashed in the paddling pool. They had played ball and Hide-and-Seek. Now, they were happy to sit in the warm sunshine, nibbling biscuits, drinking squash and chatting to each other.

Suddenly, Billy said: "We won't be doing this tomorrow!"

"Or the next day!" added Bella, biting on a biscuit.

"Or the day after!" Billy went on. "We'll be at school!"

"I'm going to school tomorrow!"
cried Teddy. "Mummy Bear's
bought me a satchel and a lunch-
box and a pencil-case, and..."
"Poor you!" said Bella.
"Never mind!" added Billy.

Teddy blinked. He had been with Mummy and Daddy Bear to see Teacher Bear's school. It seemed a very nice place to be.

"Why?" he asked at last. "What's wrong with school?"

"No sweets!" said Bella.

"You can't take any toys!" added Billy. "Or talk to your friends! And, as for school dinners…"

"YUK!" shuddered Bella. "They're really horrible!"

Just then, Billy and Bella's daddy
came to take them home, so Teddy
couldn't ask any more questions
about school. He had really thought
he would like it. Now, he wasn't
so sure.

Mummy saw how worried Teddy
was. "You'll love Teacher Bear's
School," she said. "Just wait and
see!" Teddy felt better then.
Mummy Bear never said anything
that wasn't true.

Next morning, Mummy packed Teddy's lunch-box.

"No sweets, Teddy," she said. "Teacher Bear doesn't like them being brought to school." Teddy pulled a face.

"Cheer up!" smiled Mummy. You
can have an apple and some crisps,
instead."
"Put that toy down, Teddy!" called
Daddy Bear. "Then we'll be off on
our way."

"No sweets. No toys. That's what Billy and Bella told me," thought Teddy with a sigh.

"Hello, Teddy!" a voice called. It was Barry Bear, one of Teddy's best friends.

Teddy waved and smiled.

"You'll see Barry at playtime," said Daddy Bear. "He's older than you Teddy, so he won't be in your class."

Teddy didn't like the sound of that.

"Teddy Bear!" came a voice. "Lovely to see you!" It was Teacher Bear. "Hang your coat on this peg, the one with the picture of an engine. Do you like engines?" Teddy nodded.

"Then I want you to help Barbara feed the goldfish," Teacher Bear went on.
Barbara Bear smiled at Teddy.
"I'll show you what to do, Teddy," she said.

Then Teddy sat at the table next to Honey Bear, while the drawing things were being given out. Barry Bear's mummy was there too, sorting out lids from jam pots and coffee jars.

Soon Teddy was drawing round the lids, making a picture of a lovely bunch of balloons!

"I'm going to draw lots of trees!" said Tiny Bear. "Will you help me please, Teddy?"

And when all the lunch-boxes were opened, nobody minded about not having any sweets.

"Teacher Bear says fruit and crisps are better for your teeth," explained Barry Bear.

There was time for games in the
playground, too.
Teddy loved climbing up the slide
into a little hut, crawling through
and then sliding down the other
side.

Later on, he filled lots of paper cups with sand from the sand tray, ready to weigh them on the classroom scales. And what a lovely smell there was, coming from the school kitchen!

"Dinner time!" called Teacher Bear,
ringing a little bell.

"Cheese and tomato pizza!" cried
Teddy, sniffing hungrily. And he ate
every bit, followed by some cool,
strawberry jelly.

After dinner, Teddy's class went into the play room. What toys there were! Puzzles and bricks, tricycles, push-along toys, balls, trains.... There was no need to bring toys from home!

Teddy and his friends had just finished a big jigsaw when Teacher Bear clapped her hands.

"Storytime!" she cried. "Put away the toys, then we'll go back to the classroom."

Teacher Bear had a lovely, big
story-book with lots of pictures
for everyone to see. Then they
sang songs and nursery rhymes,
clapping their hands in time to
the music.

And when Teacher Bear said it was
time to go home, Teddy thought
about all the things he had done. He
remembered the lovely dinner and
the fun he'd had with all his new
friends.

"Why did you say that you didn't like school?" he asked Billy on the way home.
"We said there were no sweets!" grinned Billy. "And that's true!"

"We said we couldn't bring toys!"
said Bella. "But we never said we
didn't LIKE school!" And they ran
off laughing. Teddy laughed too. He
knew he would see them at school
next day.

YANKEE DOODLE

Yankee Doodle came to town,
Riding on a pony,
He stuck a feather in his cap,
And called it macaroni.

MULTIPLICATION

Multiplication is vexation,
Division is as bad;
The rule of three perplexes me,
And fractions drive me mad.

CHRISTMAS IS COMING

Christmas is coming,
The geese are getting fat,
Please to put a penny
In the old man's hat.

If you haven't got a penny,
A ha'penny will do;
If you haven't got a ha'penny,
Then God bless you.

ROSES ARE RED

Roses are red,
Violets are blue,
Sugar is sweet
And so are you.

MARCH WINDS

March winds and April showers
Bring forth May flowers.

BYE, BABY BUNTING

Bye, Baby Bunting,
Daddy's gone a-hunting,
Gone to get a rabbit skin
To wrap the Baby Bunting in.

HERE WE GO ROUND THE MULBERRY BUSH

Here we go round the mulberry bush,
The mulberry bush, the mulberry bush,
Here we go round the mulberry bush,
On a cold and frosty morning.

THE QUEEN OF HEARTS

The Queen of Hearts
She made some tarts,
All on a summer's day;
The Knave of Hearts
He stole the tarts,
And took them right away.

The King of Hearts
Called for the tarts,
And beat the Knave full sore;
The Knave of Hearts
Brought back the tarts,
And vowed he'd steal no more.

PETER, PETER, PUMPKIN EATER

Peter, Peter, Pumpkin Eater,
Had a wife and couldn't keep her;
He put her in a pumpkin shell,
And there he kept her very well.

Peter, Peter, Pumpkin Eater,
Had another and didn't love her;
Peter learned to read and spell,
And then he loved her very well.

THIS LITTLE COW EATS GRASS

This little cow eats grass,
This little cow eats hay.
This little cow drinks water,
This little cow runs away.

This little cow does nothing,
Except lie down all day.
We'll chase her,
We'll chase her,
We'll chase her away!

Index